W9-CPE-580

NOV 2018

DISNEY
RALPH BREAKS THE INTERNET

GAME TIME!

by Susan Amerikaner

illustrated by the Disney Storybook Art Team

Random House 🏠 New York

Wreck-It Ralph wrecks things
in the *Fix-It Felix Jr.*
video game.
Vanellope races cars
in the *Sugar Rush* game.
They are best friends.
Ralph is Vanellope's hero.

Sugar Rush needs

a new steering wheel.

The only place to get it is at eBay,

a shop on the Internet.

Ralph and Vanellope go
inside the Internet.
Ralph thinks it is scary.
Vanellope thinks it is fun!

They must get
to eBay fast—
or *Sugar Rush* will shut
down forever!

Ralph and Vanellope arrive
at eBay just in time
to get the steering wheel.
But they have to pay for it.
They do not have any money!

They learn that to make money,
they must find special objects
in video games.
They can sell the objects
and buy the steering wheel!

Vanellope and Ralph go
to an exciting racing game.
Shank is the best racer.
Her car is fancy and fast!

If Ralph and Vanellope get it,
they will make enough money
to buy the steering wheel.
They take Shank's car!
Shank sees that Vanellope
is a good driver.
But Shank is better.
She stops them.

Shank and her gang make
Ralph look silly.
A video of Ralph's funny face
goes on the Internet.
People everywhere see it.

Shank tells Vanellope
she is a good driver.
Vanellope is happy.
She thinks Shank's
racing game is super cool!

Ralph and Vanellope meet a lady named Yesss.

Yesss explains that they can earn the money they need by making videos.

People like Ralph's video.

They give it hearts.

Hearts mean money!

Yesss asks Ralph to make

more videos to get more hearts—

and make more money.

Ralph is happy to do it!

Ralph's new videos get

lots of hearts.

He makes lots of money.

He buys the steering wheel!

He calls Vanellope

to tell her the good news.

Vanellope misses Ralph's call.

But Ralph can hear her.

Vanellope tells Shank

she wants to stay

in her racing game.

Ralph does not want her

to stay with Shank.

Ralph's pal Spamley takes him
to meet Double Dan.
Dan has a virus worm that
can slow down Shank's game.
It will make the game less fun.

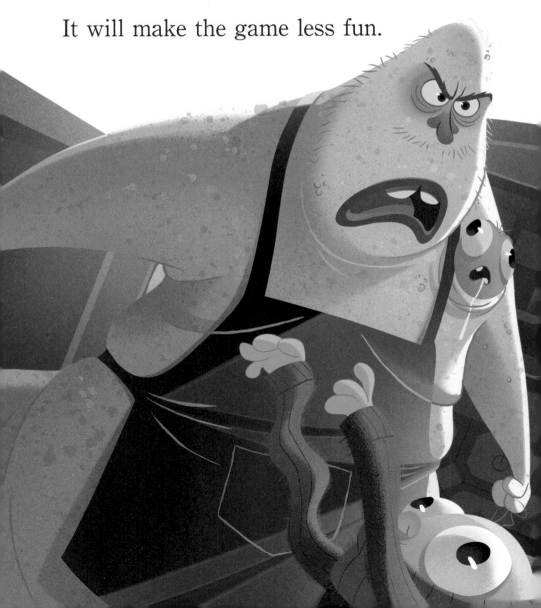

Then Vanellope will want to go
back to *Sugar Rush*!
Double Dan puts the virus worm
in an envelope.
He warns Ralph not to let it
leave Shank's racing game
and go into the Internet!

Ralph puts the envelope
in Vanellope's race car.
Vanellope thinks it is a nice
note from Shank.
She opens it.
The virus worm escapes!

Vanellope's car crashes.

Ralph takes her out of the game.

The envelope falls out of

Vanellope's pocket.

Ralph does not see it fall.

The virus goes into the Internet!

Ralph admits it is his fault

that Shank's game

is broken.

Vanellope is mad at Ralph.

She wants to go back

to Shank's game.

Now the virus worm is in the Internet!

It is making clones

that look just like Ralph.

The Ralph clones are wrecking

the Internet!

Ralph and Vanellope go
into the Internet.
They must stop
the virus!

Yesss tries to help them,
but there are too many clones.
They are forming
one giant Ralph!

The giant Ralph clone grabs
Ralph and Vanellope.
Ralph is scared.
Vanellope tries to make Ralph
feel better.

Vanellope tells Ralph that she
will always be his best friend,
no matter where she goes.
Friendship is a good feeling.
Ralph's good feelings make
the giant Ralph clone go away!

The Internet is safe again.
Vanellope still wants to return
to Shank's racing game.

Ralph will miss her,
but he understands that
it is Vanellope's dream.

Ralph and Vanellope
say goodbye.
Ralph returns to wrecking things
in his game.
Vanellope stays in the Internet.

They are both doing
what they love.

They will always be
best friends.
And Ralph will always be
Vanellope's hero!

Step into Reading, Random House, and the Random House colophon are registered trademarks
of Penguin Random House LLC.

Visit us on the Web!
StepIntoReading.com
rhcbooks.com

Educators and librarians, for a variety of teaching tools, visit us at RHTeachersLibrarians.com

ISBN 978-0-7364-3757-8 (trade) — ISBN 978-0-7364-8258-5 (lib. bdg.)
ISBN 978-0-7364-3758-5 (ebook)

Printed in the United States of America   10 9 8 7 6 5 4 3 2 1

Dear Parents:

Congratulations! Your child is taking the first steps on an exciting journey. The destination? Independent reading!

STEP INTO READING® will help your child get there. The program offers five steps to reading success. Each step includes fun stories and colorful art or photographs. In addition to original fiction and books with favorite characters, there are Step into Reading Non-Fiction Readers, Phonics Readers and Boxed Sets, Sticker Readers, and Comic Readers—a complete literacy program with something to interest every child.

Learning to Read, Step by Step!

Ready to Read   Preschool–Kindergarten
• big type and easy words • rhyme and rhythm • picture clues
For children who know the alphabet and are eager to begin reading.

Reading with Help   Preschool–Grade 1
• basic vocabulary • short sentences • simple stories
For children who recognize familiar words and sound out new words with help.

Reading on Your Own   Grades 1–3
• engaging characters • easy-to-follow plots • popular topics
For children who are ready to read on their own.

Reading Paragraphs   Grades 2–3
• challenging vocabulary • short paragraphs • exciting stories
For newly independent readers who read simple sentences with confidence.

Ready for Chapters   Grades 2–4
• chapters • longer paragraphs • full-color art
For children who want to take the plunge into chapter books but still like colorful pictures.

STEP INTO READING® is designed to give every child a successful reading experience. The grade levels are only guides; children will progress through the steps at their own speed, developing confidence in their reading.

Remember, a lifetime love of reading starts with a single step!